Hilmy *the* Hippo

Learns to be grateful

Rae Norridge

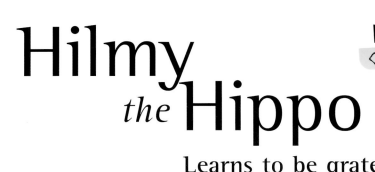

The Islamic Foundation

Hilmy was a large, happy hippo who lived at a quiet water hole. One day he decided that the water hole was too small for a hippo as grand as himself.

2

So, one morning,
after a hearty breakfast of reeds,
Hilmy said goodbye to his best
friend the blue dragonfly,

and set off in search of another water hole.

3

He hadn't walked far when he met Stripe, the zebra.
Hilmy greeted Stripe with a cheery, *"As-Salamu 'Alaykum."*

"Wa 'Alaykum as-Salam," replied Stripe.
"Why are you so far from home, Hilmy?"

4

"I need a far grander place to live now," said Hilmy. "A quiet water hole is for small frogs and fish and not for the likes of a fine hippo such as myself." "I wish you good luck," replied Stripe the zebra raising his eyebrows. "*Ma' Salamah* Hilmy."

Hilmy went on his way.

5

It was late in the afternoon when Hilmy
found a beautiful pond filled with water lilies.
Subhanallah! thought Hilmy, just the sort of
place I'm looking for.

6

Hilmy ambled across the sandy bank and plunged into the cool water. He romped and played, splashing the water all around him.

Suddenly Hilmy heard a strange noise. He slipped under the water and listened. He heard the noise again.

Slowly and quietly he popped his eyes and ears out of the water.

8

To Hilmy's amazement he saw that many elephants had come down to the water hole to drink and bathe.

Hilmy was very frightened. He was alone, in the middle of all the elephants splashing and playing in the water, which had soon been turned into mud.

When the elephants had finished bathing, Hilmy quickly left the pond.

9

Further along the way,
he met Stork.

"*As-Salamu 'Alaykum*, Stork,"
said Hilmy. "Do you know where
I can find a nice water hole?"

"*Wa 'Alaykum as-Salam*," replied Stork.
"Yes, I know a very nice lake, but it is a
long way from here.

10

You must cross the mountain.
The lake is on the other side."

Hilmy was very pleased to hear
this and thanked his good
friend Stork. He then hurried
on his way.

The mountain was very big.
It took Hilmy all day to climb up the mountain
and all of the next day to climb down the other side.

The lake was just as Stork had said; it was very beautiful.
The water sparkled in the morning sun.

12

Hilmy ran down to the water's edge shouting, "*Al-Hamdulillah*!" He plunged into the water and splashed about as hippos do. He was having fun.

"Excuse me, but, who are you?"

13

Hilmy looked up and saw a very, very large hippo.

"My name is Hilmy and I want to live in this lake," he replied happily.

"This is our lake Hilmy," said the large hippo in a stern voice. "You cannot live here. We found the lake first and there is no room for any more hippos."

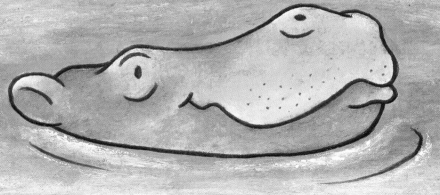

Looking around, Hilmy felt scared. He saw lots of hippos. Some were basking in the sun on the sandy banks of the lake, while others were wallowing in the water.

Hilmy looked at the large hippo and in a brave
voice said, "This is a nice lake and it is big
enough for all of us. But since you are so unkind
I do not wish to have you as my neighbour."

  With this, Hilmy left the water and went sadly on his way.

15

He hadn't walked very far when he found another nice but smaller lake. Water lilies covered the surface of the water and shady fig trees grew on the banks. *Subhanallah*! What a beautiful sight. Hilmy was very pleased.

Once again Hilmy slipped into the cool water. Instead of splashing about, he rested in the water with only his eyes and ears above the surface.

Suddenly, Hilmy noticed the water lilies beginning to move. It was a crocodile. Hilmy swam away from it only to find another one, and then another and another.

This is not for me, thought Hilmy; I must find another place to live.

Once again Hilmy set out to find yet another water hole.
He soon met Giraffe.

"*As-Salamu 'Alaykum*," called Hilmy. "It is a lovely day
today, Giraffe. Maybe you can tell me where I can
find a nice water hole?"

"Yes, I do know a lovely water hole. In fact," said Giraffe,
"It is the prettiest water hole I have ever seen. It has plenty
of tall, juicy reeds for you to eat.

18

No crocodiles live at the water hole, and it is too small for a herd of elephants to bathe. *Insha' Allah* it will be just perfect for you Hilmy."

"Please show me the way to this water hole," pleaded Hilmy.

"First you climb up the mountain and down the other side. Then you must follow the path towards the setting sun. When you pass the large baobab tree you will find the water hole."

Hilmy set off immediately. He climbed up the mountain. The next day he climbed down the other side. He followed the path towards the setting sun and passed the large baobab tree.

And there, to Hilmy's amazement, was his very own water hole. His best friend Dragonfly hovered above the shiny surface of the water.

"Welcome home, Hilmy," called Dragonfly.
"Thank you," replied Hilmy, "It is good to
be back home."

Yes, thought Hilmy. This is a beautiful pond,
plenty of reeds for me to eat. There are no
crocodiles or elephants. It is quiet and peaceful.

"Why did you leave this water hole?" asked Dragonfly.

"I left because I went in search of something better, because I thought that this water hole was not good enough for me," said Hilmy. "But my search has taught me that although there are bigger and better water holes, this water hole is just right for me."

"Allah has been kind to you Hilmy,"
replied Dragonfly. "He brought you back home."

"It is good to be back home. *Al-Hamdulillah*!"
sighed Hilmy. "**Thank you Allah!**"

23

As-Salamu 'Alaykum:
Literally "Peace be upon you",
the traditional Muslim greeting,
offered when Muslims meet
each other.

Wa 'Alaykum as-Salam:
"Peace be upon you too"
is the reply to the greeting,
expressing their mutual love,
sincerity and best wishes.

Ma' Salamah:
Literally "with peace",
the traditional Muslim farewell
offered when Muslims depart
from each other.

Al-Hamdulillah:
Literally "Praise be to Allah".
It is used for expressing thanks
and gratefulness to Allah. This
supplication is also used when one
sneezes, in order to thank Allah for
having relieved discomfort out of
His boundless mercy.

Subhanallah:
Literally "Glory be to Allah".
It reflects a Muslim's appreciation
and amazement at observing any
manifestation of Allah's greatness.

Insha' Allah:
Literally "If Allah so wishes".
Used by Muslims to indicate their
decision to do something, provided
they get help from Allah. It is
recommended that whenever
Muslims resolve to do something
and make a promise, they should
add "Insha' Allah".